STEP INTO READING®

STEP 3

W9-DCM-212

Beans Baker Bounces Back

by Richard Torrey

Random House New York

"Two more hops and you'll have
the Robo-Pogo record, Beans!"
cried Chester.
"Forty, forty-one, forty-two . . . ,"
counted Lindsay.

"You did it!"

Everyone cheered.

Beans was still smiling
when he got home.
"You're looking at the
Robo-Pogo champion
of the universe!"
Beans said proudly.

6

"That's nice, champ,"
said his mother.
"Now please start your homework.
And don't forget to study
your spelling words."
"Oh, Mom," groaned Beans.

The next morning,
everyone was talking
about Beans's Robo-Pogo record.
"I knew he could do it,"
said Chester.
"After all, he *is* my best friend."

"Wow! I'm walking with
a real record holder,"
said Molly Mall.
"I'll give you my cookies
if you teach me to pogo,"
said Russell.

But at recess,

Sheldon set a new record.

"Fifty hops!" shouted Chester.

"That's amazing.

Don't you think so, Beans?"

"Amazing," said Beans.

"Hey, Sheldon,
I'll give you my cookies
if you teach me to pogo,"
said Russell.

11

Suddenly all Beans could
think about was winning
back his record.
He practiced all afternoon.

After dinner, Beans raced
through his spelling homework.

Then he grabbed his Robo-Pogo
to practice some more.
"Did you study for your
spelling test?" asked his mother.
"Tomorrow's test is
just for practice," said Beans.
"The real test isn't
until next week!"

"Practice makes perfect,"
said Beans's father.
"And everyone with a
perfect score on the real test
gets to go to Monkey Bob's
Pizza Adventureland,"
said Beans's mother.

"Sounds hard,"

said his sister, Kitt.

"Do I look worried?" asked Beans.

"No, you look weird," said Kitt.

15

The next day at recess, Beans
tied Sheldon's Robo-Pogo record.

But in class, Beans did poorly
on the practice test.
He spelled every word wrong
except one: *disaster*.

"I can't believe I got an F,"
said Beans after school.

Beans thought his day
could not get any worse.
But then Sheldon came
stomping up the stairs.

"It's time we find out
   who the best Robo-Pogo-er is,"
snarled Sheldon.
"I challenge you to a
   Robo-Pogo contest."

"Great idea!" said Lindsay.

"Whoever wins will be

Champion for Life!"

"And whoever loses will be

Loser for Life!" sneered Sheldon.

"That means you!"

21

The contest would be
in one week.
Sheldon pointed
at Beans.
"And if you weasel out, I win!"
he snarled.

"Don't worry, Beans," said Lindsay.

"You'll beat him!"

"That's if my parents don't
take away my Robo-Pogo
when they see this F," said Beans.

"I should have studied
harder," said Beans.
"I'm sorry."
"Not as sorry as you'll be
when you don't go
to Monkey Bob's," said Kitt.
"I'm going to Monkey Bob's!"
Beans promised.
"I'm going to ace the *real* test!"

"That means more studying,"
said his mother.
"Maybe we should put the
Robo-Pogo away
until the test is over."

Then Beans told his parents about his contest with Sheldon.
It was on the same day as the test!

"If I back out, he wins!" he cried.

Suddenly Kitt had an idea.

"Put your trust in Coach Kitt!"
she said.

"I'm doomed," said Beans.

"The last word on your spelling list
is *crazy*," said Kitt the next day.
"Now hop to it!"
"I must have been *crazy*
to let you talk me into this,"
said Beans.

He started hopping on his Robo-Pogo.

"C, *(hop)* R, *(hop)* A, *(hop)*

Z, *(hop)* Y, *(hop)*" spelled Beans.

"Crazy!"

"What's he doing?" asked Chester.

"Beats me," said Lindsay.

"Good," said Kitt.

"Let's try all twenty words again.

And remember,

if you misspell any,

you have to start over."

"HELP!" cried Beans.

"Is that one of our spelling words?"
asked Chester.

The morning of the big day,
Beans was nervous.
"You'll do just fine,"
said his mother.
"Thanks," said Beans.

"Make your coach proud," said Kitt.

She punched Beans's arm

for good luck.

"I'll try," he squeaked.

33

At recess, everyone met
in the playground.
"LET'S GET READY TO
ROBO-POGO!" shouted Lindsay.
"On your mark, get set, go!"
"You're *(hop)* going *(hop)*
to *(hop)* lose!" snarled Sheldon.

But Beans wasn't listening.

"*Focus*," he said to himself.

"F, *(hop)* O, *(hop)* C, *(hop)* . . ."

He kept going, spelling out

the test words in his head.

"Fifty-one!" shouted Lindsay.

"You're both over the record!"

"Go, Beans!" cried Chester.

Then Sheldon bumped into Beans.

Beans tilted to the left.

He wobbled to the right.

CRASH—down he went!

Sheldon made two more hops
before he stopped.

"I'm Champion for Life!" he shouted.

"No fair!" said Lindsay.

Just then the bell rang.

"See you later, loser!"

Sheldon sneered.

"Don't listen to him, Beans,"

said Chester.

He and Lindsay helped Beans up.

"You're still the Robo-Pogo champion

to me," said Molly Mall.

"Thanks," said Beans.

Beans barely had time
to catch his breath
before the test.
"Clear your desks,"
said Mr. Munhall.
"The first spelling word is:
important."

"The whole test is important,"
thought Beans.

Suddenly his mind went blank.

He couldn't think.

He couldn't spell.

He was so nervous, he started
hopping up and down in his seat.
All at once
the letters came to him!

"I, *(hop)* M, *(hop)* P, *(hop)* . . . ,"

he spelled to himself.

"*Important!*"

Beans hopped his way through

the whole test.

Beans's test came back
with a perfect score.
"Yippee!" he cried.
"Pepperoni pizza—here we come!"
"You've earned it!"
said Mr. Munhall.

Everyone headed to

Monkey Bob's Pizza Adventureland.

Everyone except Sheldon.

He had spelled every word wrong

except one: *disaster*.

"I can't believe we're here!"
Russell whispered.
"Look at it!" shouted Chester.
"Pizza and video games
as far as the eye can see!"

"Isn't it great?" cried Lindsay.

"It's everything I *hopped* for!" said Beans.

48